ERTER

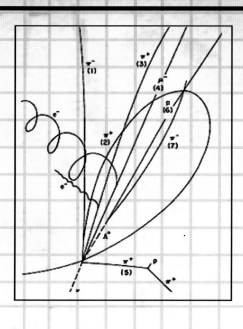

VENT

SMALL
HADRON
COLLIDER

BACKUP POWER

NUCLEAR POWER
CONTAINMENT UNIT

PASSING A CURRENT THROUGH AN IMPROVISED MICHELSON-MORLEY DEVICE WILL MINIMIZE COUNTER-RADIATION AND INHIBIT ENTROPY. PARAMETRIC DOWN-CONVERSION SHOULD COMMENCE NO LATER THAN SIX SECONDS AFTER INITIATION OF THE NIMTZ SEQUENCE TO ELIMINATE RISK OF A LAMB SHIFT. TIME DILATION MAY OCCUR ONCE MAXIMUM VELOCITY IS REACHED.

P9-DEC-834

AFTER ACHIEVING ZERO MASS, THE CRAFT WILL "PIGGYBACK" ONTO A QUARK PARTICLE, WHICH SHOULD PROVIDE THE NECESSARY LORENTZ BOOST. THE RUBBER HULL AFFORDED BY THE PHUN TIMES KIDDIE POOL DELIVERS A TOTAL PARAMETRIC DOWN CONVERSION, ELIMINATING THE NEED FOR A COSTLY (AND BULKY) DELAYED-CHOICE QUANTUM ERASER. SPECIAL CARE MUST BE TAKEN TO ENSURE THE TIPLER CYLINDER DOES NOT OVERHEAT AND COMBUST.

MAGNETIC CHARGE BARRIER

QUARK PARTICLE y

TIME
MACHINE (x)

MASS $x = 0$

VELOCITY
$x = y$

THE TIME MACHINE -03
PROJECT BELGIUM

DISNEY • HYPERION BOOKS presents

For Jon Korn, fellow time traveler and intertemporal cartographer
—MB

For Alek, Kyle, and Leah
—DS

Text copyright © 2012 by Mac Barnett
Illustrations copyright © 2012 by Dan Santat

For information address Disney • Hyperion, 125 West End Avenue, New York, New York 10023.
First Edition, June 2012
10 9 8 7 6 5 4 3 2
FAC-005376-15156
Printed in China
Reinforced binding
Visit www.DisneyBooks.com
The illustrations were created using Adobe Photoshop. The text is set in 18-point Dantat.
Library of Congress Cataloging-in-Publication Data
Barnett, Mac.
Oh no! Not again! : (or how I built a time machine to save history) (or at least my history grade) / by Mac Barnett ; illustrated by Dan Santat.—1st ed.
p. cm.
Summary: When she does not get a perfect score on her history test, a young girl builds a time machine to remedy the situation.
ISBN 978-1-4231-4912-5
[1. Time travel—Fiction. 2. Cave paintings—Fiction. 3. Cave dwellers—Fiction. 4. Humorous stories.] I. Santat, Dan, ill. II. Title. III. Title: (How I built a time machine to save history) (Or at least my history grade).
PZ7.B266150g 2012
[E]—dc23   2011011111

OH NO! NOT AGAIN!

(OR HOW I BUILT A TIME MACHINE TO SAVE HISTORY)
(OR AT LEAST MY HISTORY GRADE)

WRITTEN BY **MAC BARNETT**   ILLUSTRATED BY **DAN SANTAT**

Disney · HYPERION BOOKS / NEW YORK

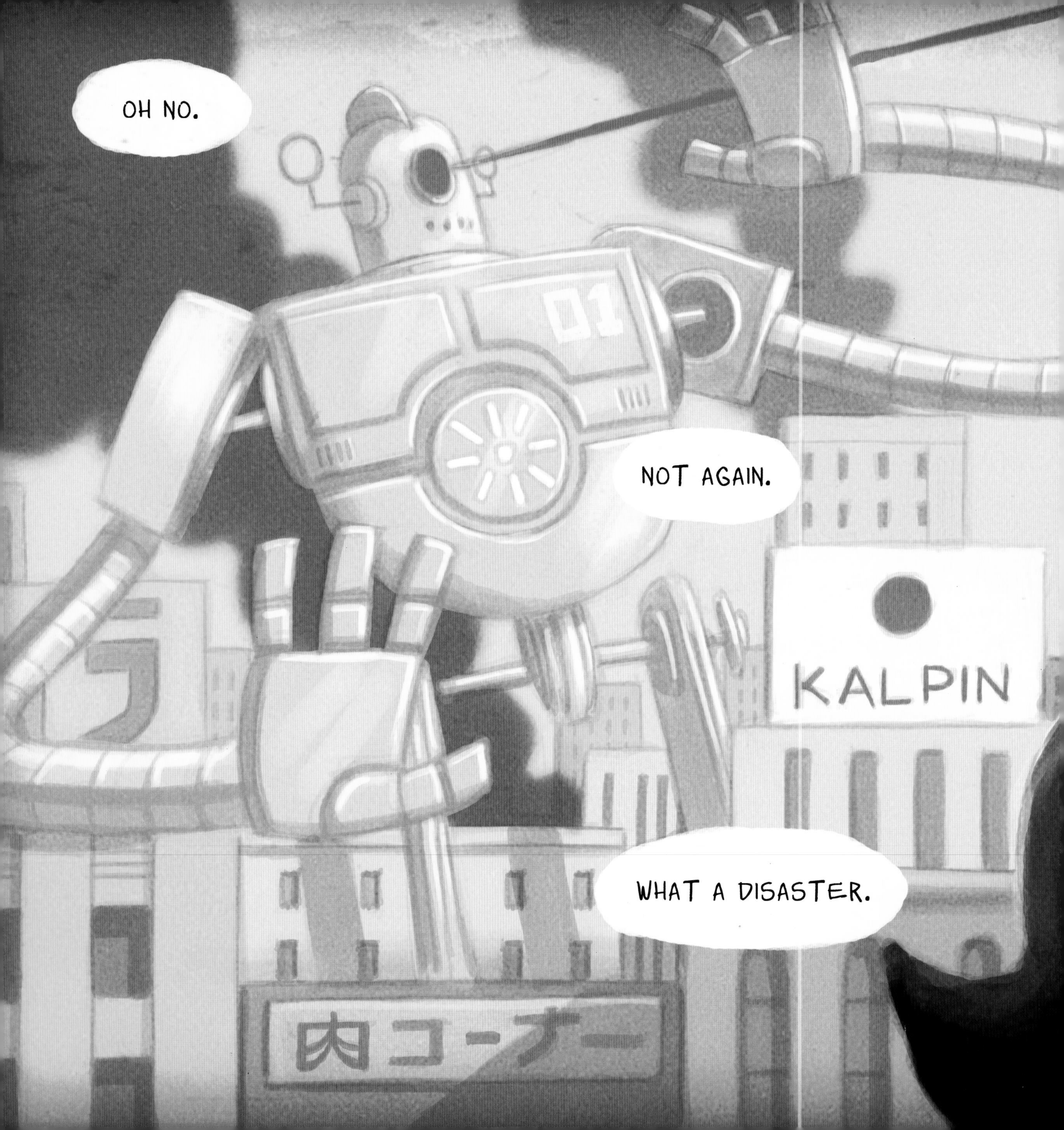
OH NO.
NOT AGAIN.
WHAT A DISASTER.
01
KALPIN
肉コーナー

I JUST NEED TO BUILD A TIME MACHINE AND CHANGE HISTORY SO I AM RIGHT.

LET'S GET THIS SHOW ON THE ROAD.

MAYBE OILS ARE NOT THEIR MEDIUM.

I SHOULD PROBABLY START WITH THE BASICS.

THERE THE WORLD'S OLDEST CAVE PAINTINGS ARE NOW IN BELGIUM.

TODAY, I'VE CHANGED A LITTLE BIT OF HISTORY.

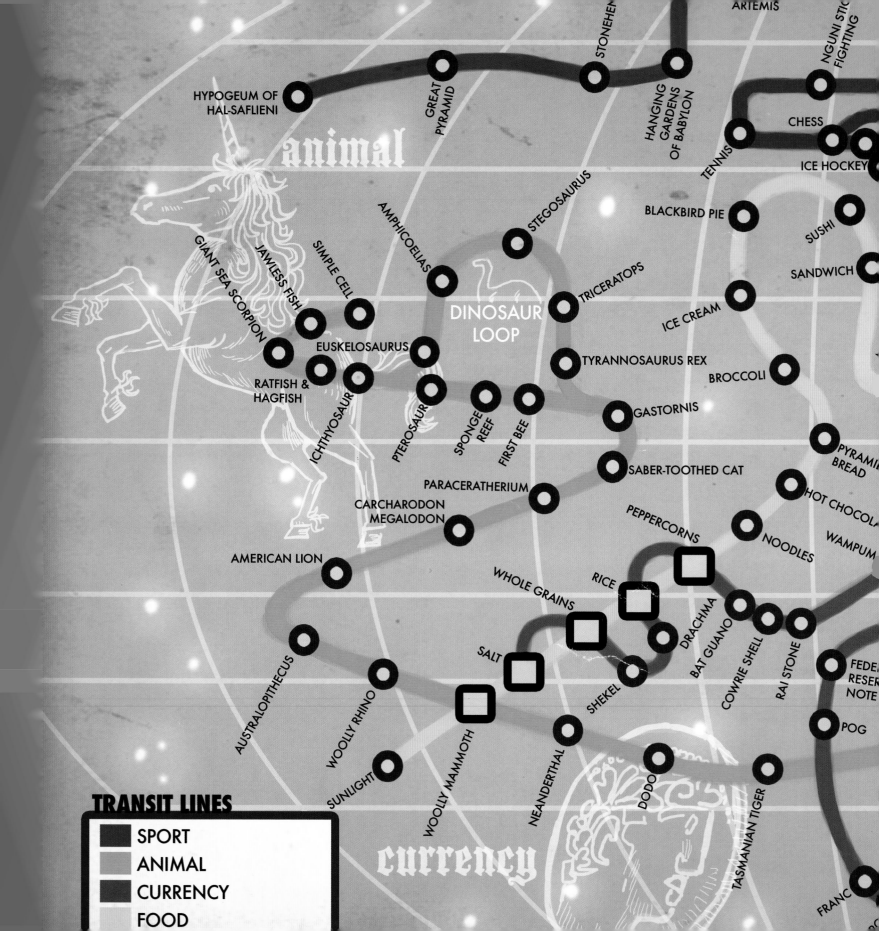

ARTEMIS

NGUNI STIC
FIGHTING

HYPOGEUM OF
HAL-SAFLIENI

GREAT
PYRAMID

STONEHENGE

HANGING
GARDENS
OF BABYLON

CHESS

TENNIS

ICE HOCKEY

animal

STEGOSAURUS

BLACKBIRD PIE

SUSHI

AMPHICOELIAS

SANDWICH

GIANT SEA SCORPION

JAWLESS FISH

SIMPLE CELL

DINOSAUR
LOOP

TRICERATOPS

ICE CREAM

EUSKELOSAURUS

TYRANNOSAURUS REX

BROCCOLI

RATFISH &
HAGFISH

ICHTHYOSAUR

PTEROSAUR

SPONGE
REEF

FIRST BEE

GASTORNIS

PYRAMID
BREAD

SABER-TOOTHED CAT

HOT CHOCOLATE

PARACERATHERIUM

PEPPERCORNS

NOODLES

WAMPUM

CARCHARODON
MEGALODON

RICE

AMERICAN LION

WHOLE GRAINS

DRACHMA

BAT GUANO

COWRIE SHELL

RAI STONE

FEDE
RESER
NOTE

AUSTRALOPITHECUS

SALT

SHEKEL

WOOLLY RHINO

POG

SUNLIGHT

WOOLLY MAMMOTH

NEANDERTHAL

DODO

TASMANIAN TIGER

FRANC

currency

TRANSIT LINES

⬛	SPORT
⬜	ANIMAL
⬛	CURRENCY
⬜	FOOD

S

HEIGHT: 5 METERS
LENGTH: 6.2 METERS
HORSEPOWER: 290 GROSS
WEIGHT: 5500 LBS
TOP SPEED: 220 KTS
EMPTY WEIGHT: 3737 LBS
CRUISE SPEED: 212 KTS
FUEL CAPACITY: 165 GAL
STALL SPEED (DIRTY): 74 KTS
RANGE: INFINITY

ENERGY CONDUIT

ZERO INER

ROLL BAR

ROLL BAR

V

FIRE EXTINGUISHER

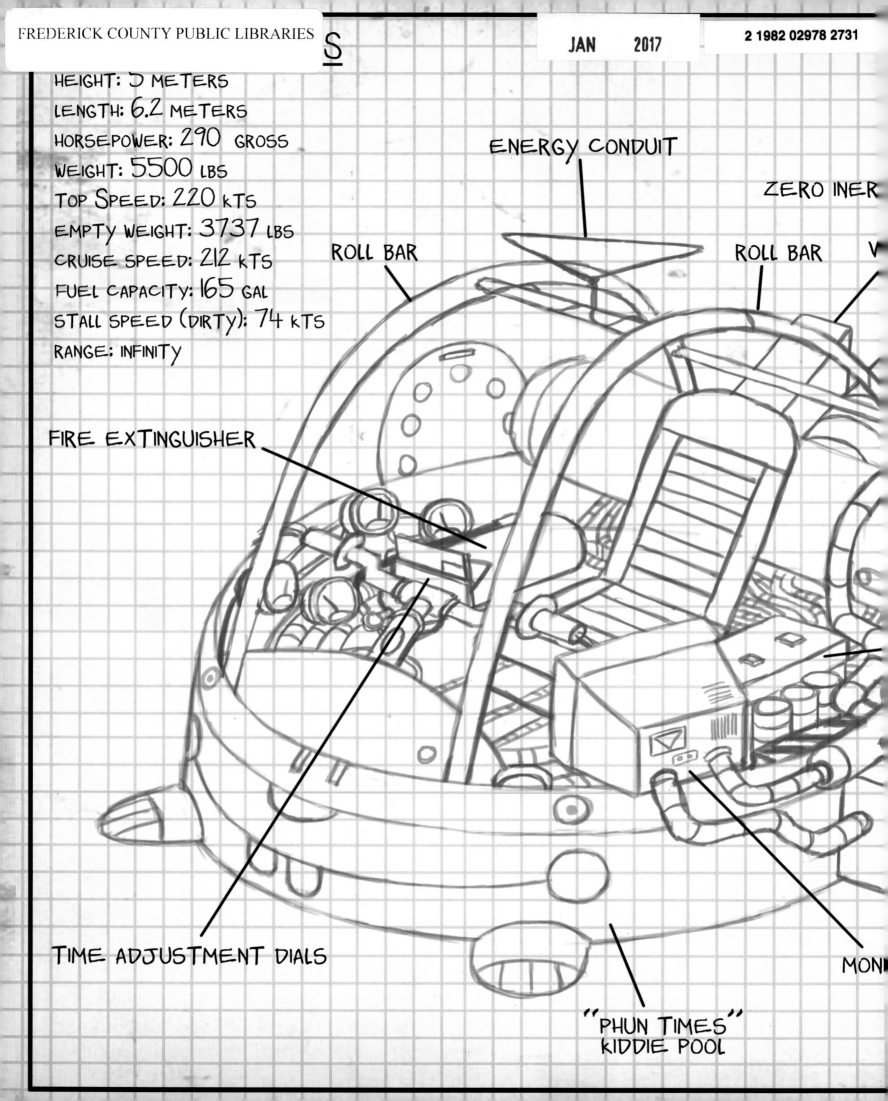

TIME ADJUSTMENT DIALS

"PHUN TIMES"
KIDDIE POOL

MON